Copyright © 2004 by Ingrid & Dieter Schubert
Originally published by Lemniscaat b.v Rotterdam
under the title *Mijn Held*
All rights reserved
Printed in Belgium
CIP data available
First U.S. edition

Ingrid & Dieter Schubert

MY Hero

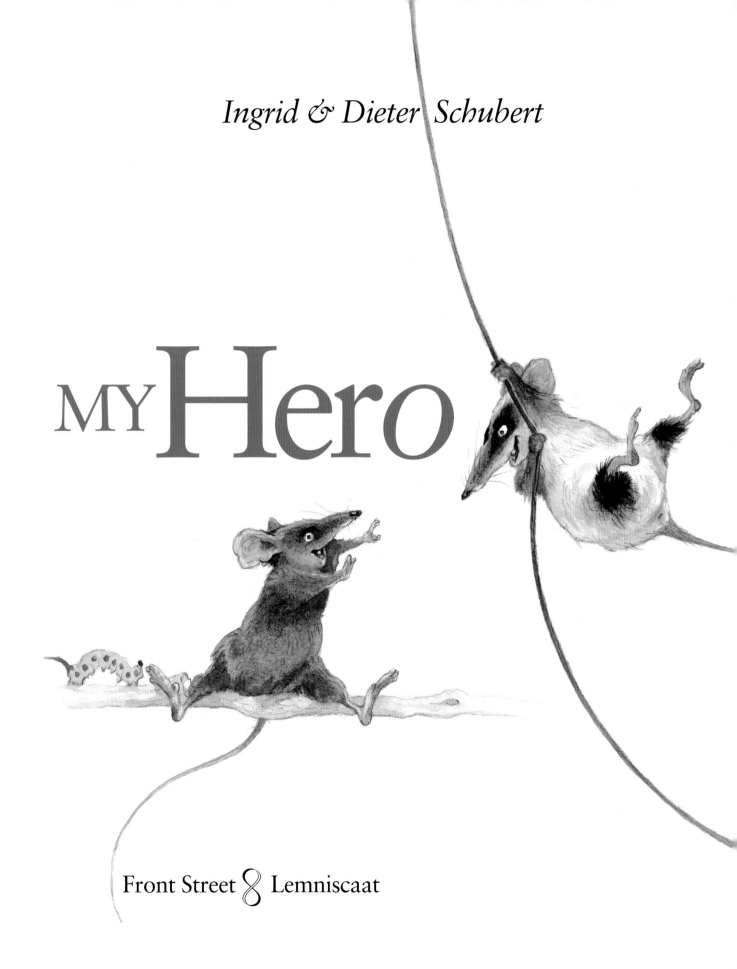

Front Street 8 Lemniscaat

High up on a branch Mouse was sitting with his
Mousegirl. He looked her deeply in the eyes and said:
 "My love for you has no barriers. Nothing can keep me
away from you. If I were here and you were on the other
side of the world, then … then…"
 "Then what?" Mousegirl asked. "What would you do?"

"I would walk around the world so I could be with you. No river is too deep, no mountain too high."

"But you would have to cross so many mountains!"

"Not a problem. I am a very good climber."

"Uphill, downhill—it will take you forever…"

"No way! I'll just throw my trusty rope from one mountaintop to another and I'll walk across it like a tight rope."

"Would you have the courage?" Sighed Mousegirl.
"Of course I would! I'll do anything for you.
Wind, rain, heat, cold—nothing can stop me. If I
have to, I'll walk in my bare feet through the snow."
"But not the desert! The sand is so hot!"

"I'll lasso a camel and ride across the desert just like that."

"And when you get to the ocean, what will you do?"

"I'll go by boat."

"But a boat can sink! If it does, what about all the scary creatures in the water? Crocodiles and sharks for instance. They'll eat you and I'll never see you again …"

"I'll catch a big fish, who will bring me safely to shore.

"As long as I have my rope, I can go anywhere
over land and across the water."
"And through the sky?"
Mouse looked at a dragonfly on the branch.
"I'll build a flying thing with wings."
"And if it crashes?"

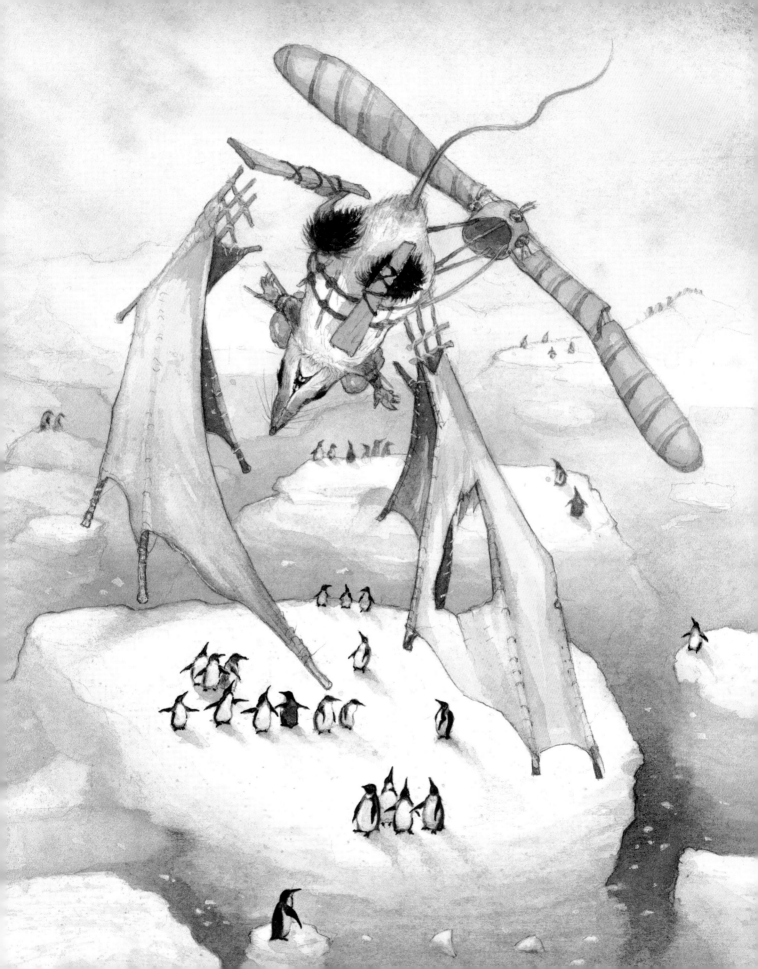

"I'll have a parachute!"

"What if I am being kidnapped" whispered Mousegirl, "would you come to rescue me?"

"I'll fight for you, of course, and when I've won, I'll tie the criminals together." Mouse blew up his chest and showed his muscles.

Suddenly they heard a craaack. The branch they were sitting on broke …

The mice fell right in front of a big, hungry-looking cat.
"What do we have hererrrre?" the cat said, purring.
Mouse dashed off like the wind.
"I'll distract him!" he squeaked hastily over his shoulder.

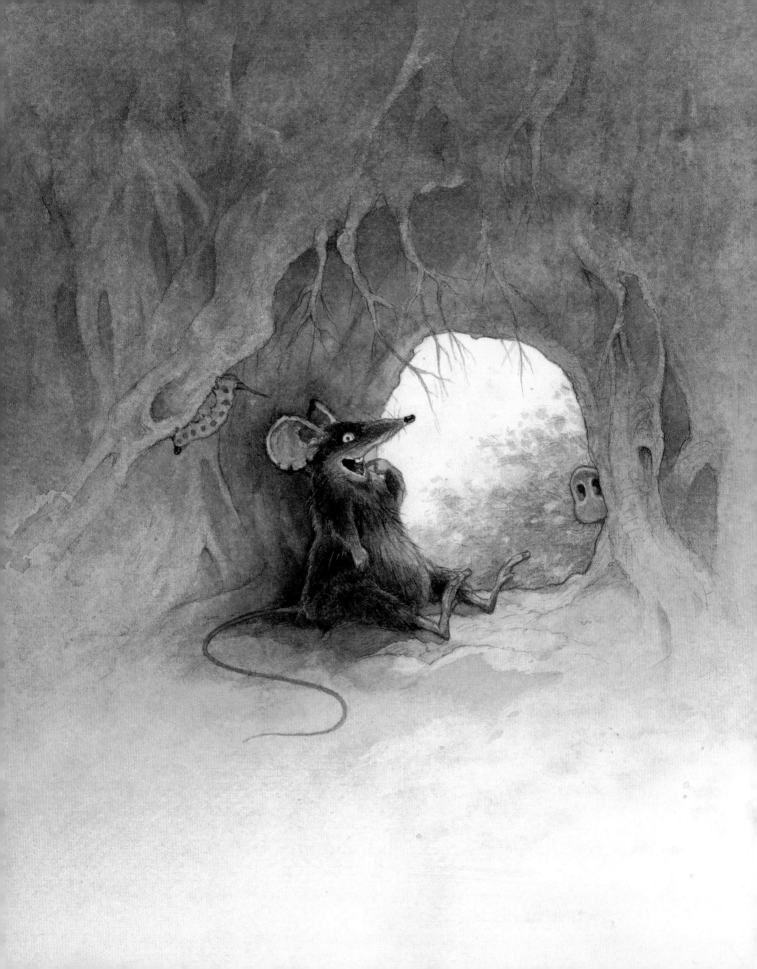

Mousegirl hid away in the nearest hole.
"My hero," she sighed, watching him. "What
a brave mouse!"

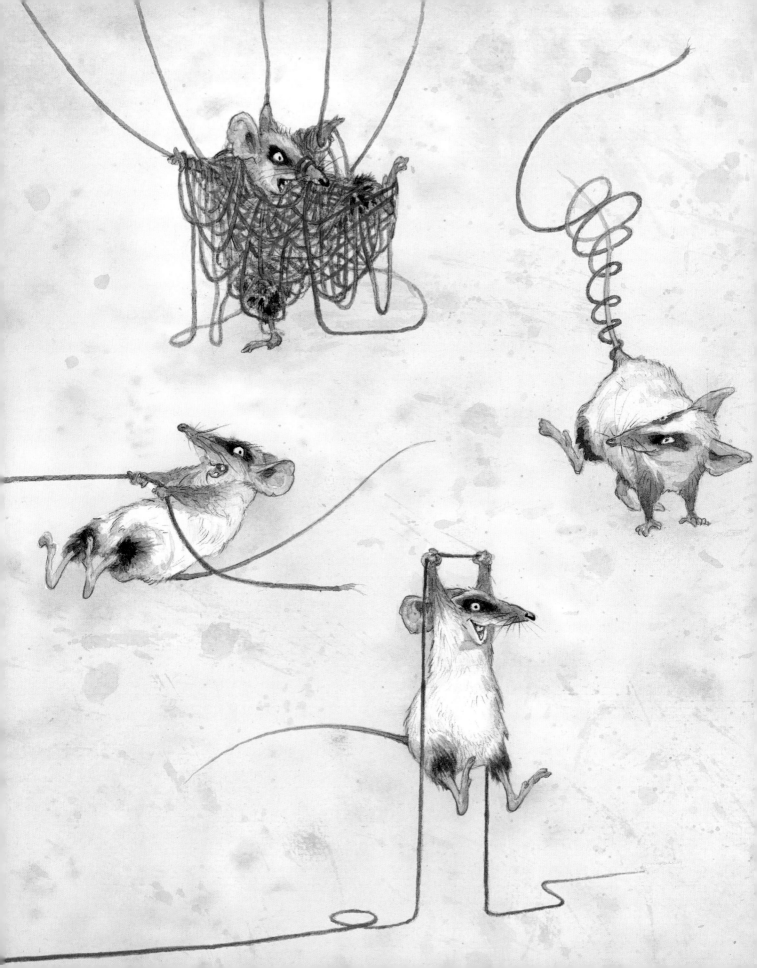